Ladybird Readers

Gus is Hot!

COVENTRY LIBRARIES
WITHDRAWN
FOR SALE

Notes to teachers, parents, and carers

The ***Ladybird Readers*** Starter Level gently introduces children to the phonics approach to reading, by covering familiar themes that young readers will have studied (for example, colors, animals, and family).

Phonics focuses on how the individual sounds of letters are blended together to sound out a word. For example, **/c/ /a/ /t/** when put together sound out the word **cat**.

The Starter Level is divided into two sub-level sections:

- **A** looks at simple words, such as **ant**, **dog**, and **red**.
- **B** explores trickier sound–letter combinations, such as the **/igh/** sound in **night** and **fright**.

This book looks at the theme of **in the sun** and focuses on these sounds and letters:
ch h u f i (long) **i** (short)

There are some activities to do in this book. They will help children practice these skills:

Spelling and writing — Speaking — Reading

LADYBIRD BOOKS

UK | USA | Canada | Ireland | Australia
India | New Zealand | South Africa

Ladybird Books is part of the Penguin Random House group of companies whose addresses can be found at global.penguinrandomhouse.com.
www.penguin.co.uk www.puffin.co.uk www.ladybird.co.uk

Penguin Random House UK

Printed in China

Paper from responsible sources
FSC® C018179

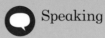

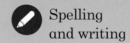

Ladybird Readers

Gus is Hot!

Look at the story

Series Editor: Sorrel Pitts
Story by Coleen Degnan-Veness
Illustrated by Chris Jevons

Picture words

Miss Tess

Ross

Gus

child

children

face

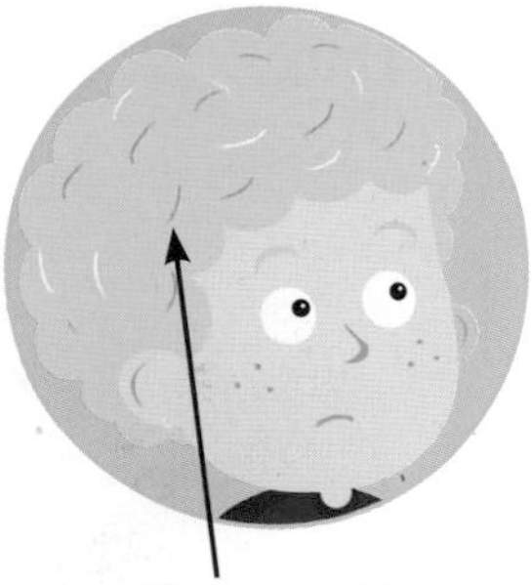
head

hot

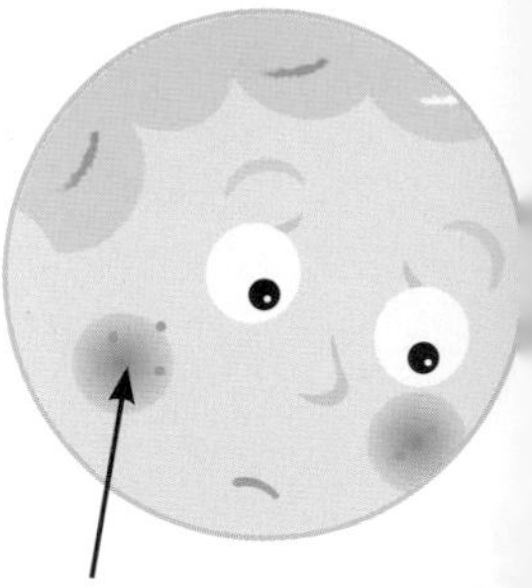
red cheeks

Aa Bb Cc Dd Ee Ff Gg Hh Ii Jj Kk Ll M

Letters and sounds: **ch h u f i** (long) **i** (short)

Theme: in the sun

net

bus

hat

catch

bugs

sun

run

sit

Use these words to help you with the activity on page 16.

Oo Pp Qq Rr Ss Tt Uu Vv Ww Xx Yy Zz

Miss Tess

net

bus

child

sit

run

sun

children

hat

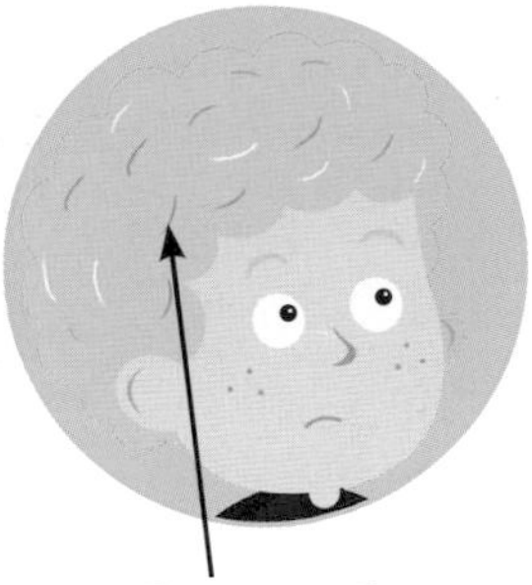

head

Gus

Ross

bugs

catch

Gus

bugs

face

sun

hot

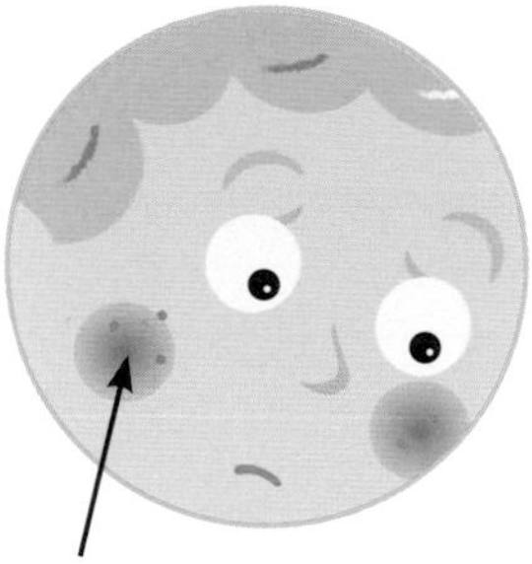

red cheeks

Activity

1 **Look. Say the sounds.**
Write the letters.

u i

1  M__i__ss Tess

2  G____s

3  ch____ld

4  r____n

Ladybird Readers

Gus is Hot!

Read the story

Miss Tess has got nets for the children.

One child is not sitting on the bus. Gus is running.

The sun is hot. The children are wearing hats.

One child has not got a hat on his head.

Ross and Gus want to catch bugs in their nets. Ross is happy.

Gus is not happy.

Ross catches lots of bugs.
Ross is happy.

Gus is not happy.
He has not got one bug.
The sun is on Gus's face.

Gus's head is hot.
He has got red cheeks.

Gus is not happy.

Activities

2 Look. Say the words. Circle the word with the same sound.

1 

b**u**s

hat bugs net

2 

cheeks

sun head child

3 

hot

run hat sit

4 

s**u**n

run net happy

5 

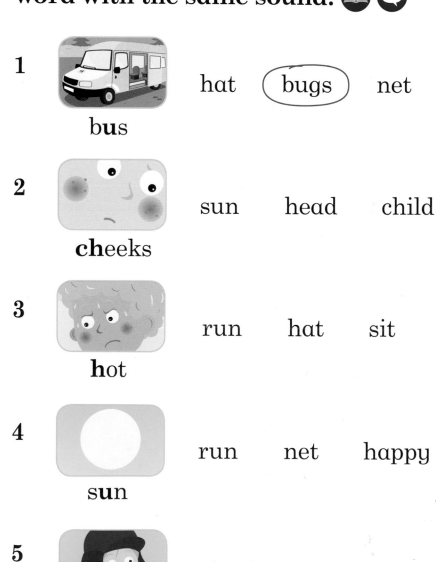

ch**i**ld

cheeks find bug

3 Look. Say the words. Put a ✓ by the words with the sound *ch*.

1  cheeks ✓

2  head ☐

3  Ross ☐

4  child ☐

5  children ☐

4 Choose the correct words, and write them on the lines. 📖 ✏️

(bug)   (Gus)   (run)

1   G u s
is not sitting.

2   He is _____ning.

3   Gus has not got one
_____ _____ _____ .

5 **What has Ross got?**

What has Gus got?

Put a ✓ in the correct boxes.

		Ross	Gus
1	hat	✓	
2	net		
3	red cheeks		
4	bugs		
5	hot head		

Starter Level A and B

978–0–241–28346–2

978–0–241–28340–0

978–0–241–28342–4

978–0–241–28343–1

978–0–241–29912–8

978–0–241–28339–4

978–0–241–28341–7

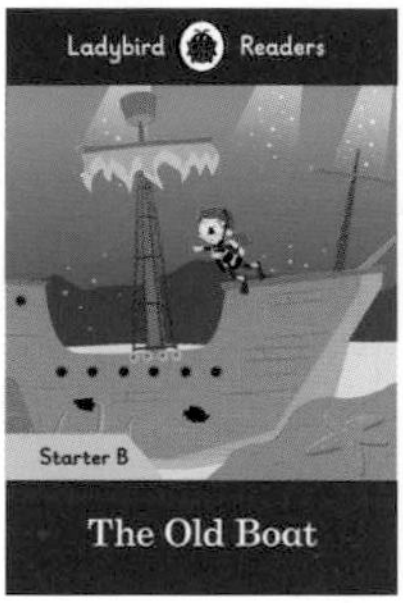

978–0–241–28345–5

978–0–241–28338–7

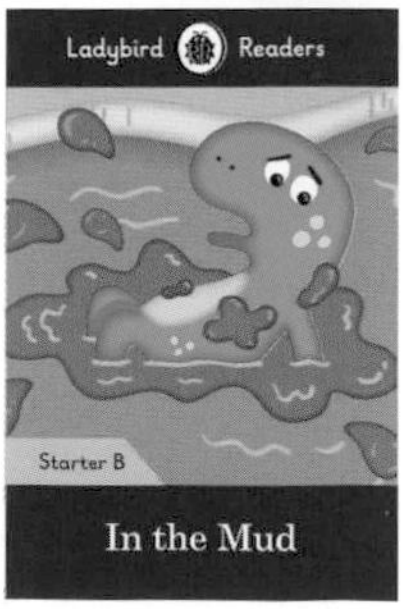

978–0–241–29913–5

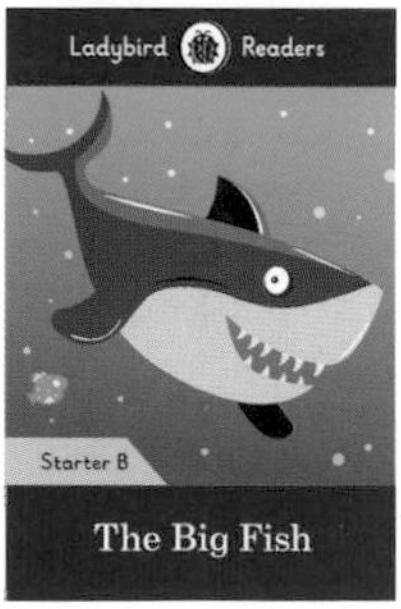

978–0–241–29915–9

978–0–241–29914–2